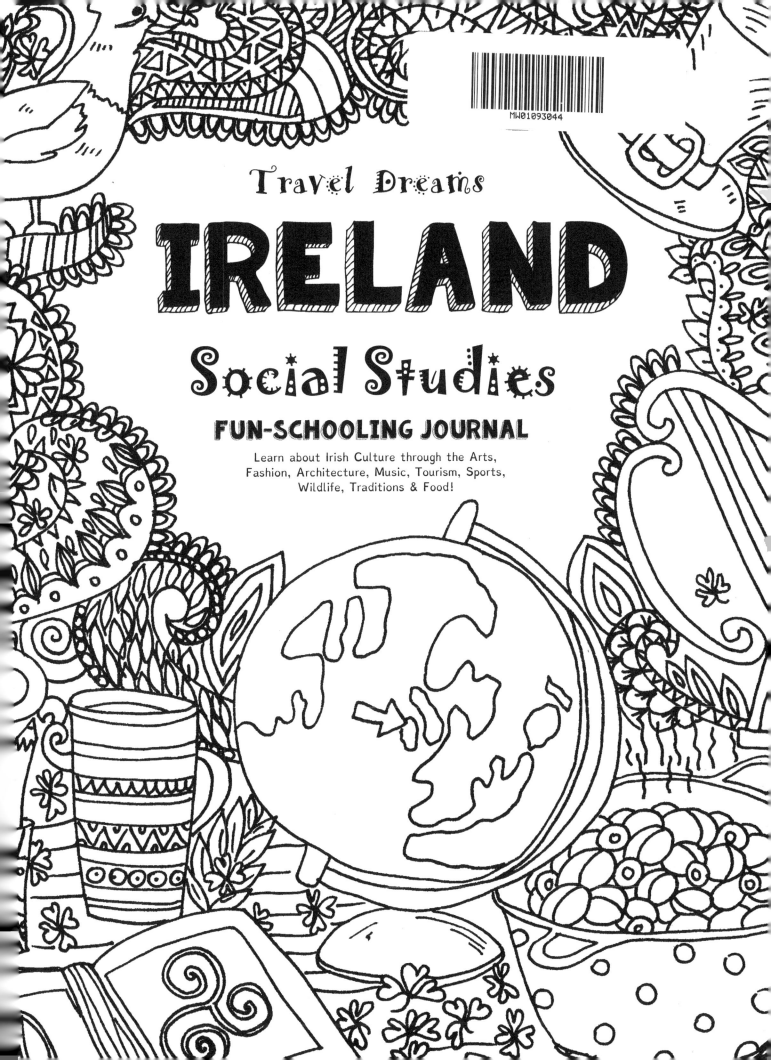

Travel Dreams

IRELAND

Social Studies

FUN-SCHOOLING JOURNAL

Learn about Irish Culture through the Arts,
Fashion, Architecture, Music, Tourism, Sports,
Wildlife, Traditions & Food!

To hear traditional music from this country listen to

Travel Dreams Geography

AROUND THE WORLD IN 14 SONGS

Search for Amazon Product Number: B072C2QXJS

Around the world in 14 songs is a delightful musical tour of the world. Adults and children will enjoy these original instrumental songs that reflect the authentic style of music that originated on all six major continents. Travel to the rhythm and melody of traditional instruments, and enjoy the fun-filled tunes.

The musical journey begins in Ireland, sweeps across Europe, dances through Asia, Africa and then soars over the ocean to Australia and the Caribbean! After an exciting night at a Smoky Mountain bluegrass festival you will enjoy a siesta in Mexico and finally land in Brazil where you will join the festa in Rio-De-Janeiro.

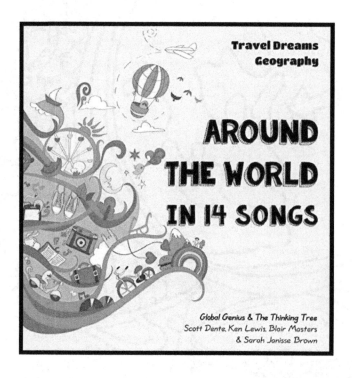

Travel Dreams Geography

AROUND THE WORLD IN 14 SONGS

Global Genius & The Thinking Tree
Scott Dente, Ken Lewis, Blair Masters
& Sarah Janisse Brown

Music has never been more fun... or educational!

2

Travel Dreams
IRELAND
FUN-SCHOOLING
JOURNAL

An Adventurous Approach
Social Studies

Learn about Irish Culture Through the Arts,
Fashion, Architecture, Music, Tourism, Sports,
Wildlife, Traditions & Food!

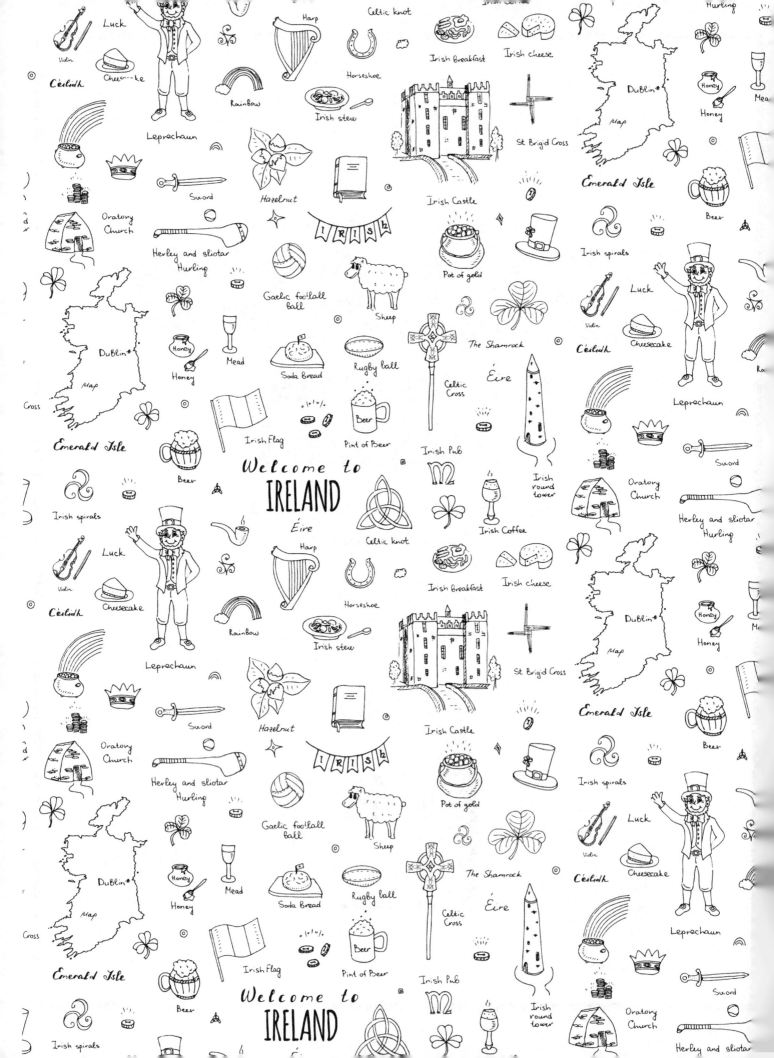

Travel Dreams
IRELAND
FUN-SCHOOLING
Journal

Name:

Date:

Contact Information:

About Me:

Let's Learn!

Topics & Activities You Can Explore With This Curriculum:

- Ethnic Cooking
- Travel
- History of Interesting Places
- How People Live
- Tourism
- Transportation
- Wildlife and Natural Wonders
- Cultural Traditions
- Natural Disasters

- Famous and Interesting People
- Missionary Stories
- Scientific Discoveries
- Fashion
- Architecture
- Plants
- Animals
- Maps
- Language

IRELAND

Travel Dreams Fun-School Journal
You are going to learn about Ireland

Teacher & Parent To-Do List:

- Plan a trip to Ireland or just plan a trip to the library or local bookstore.
- Download Google Earth so your child can zoom in and learn more!
- Choose online videos about Ireland so your child can learn about culture, food, tourism, traditions and history.
- Be prepared to help your child choose an ethnic recipe and shop for the ingredients.

Go to the Library or Bookstore to Pick Out:

- Books about Ireland
- One Atlas or Book of Maps
- One Colorful Cookbook with Recipes from Ireland

COLOR IN IRELAND ON THE MAP

Zoom into Ireland using Google Earth and explore the wonders
of this amazing country!

LABEL THE MAP
Add 15 Interesting Things to this Map!

Write or Draw
Use your Library Books

Popular Foods:	Traditional Clothing:

Draw the Flag:	A Quote or Proverb:

A Historic Event:	A Famous Landmark:

15

LEARNING TIME

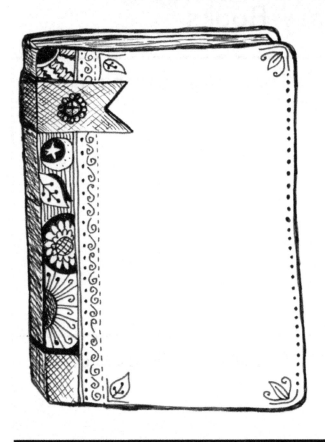

READ A BOOK AND WATCH A VIDEO ABOUT FOOD IN IRELAND:

BOOK TITLE:_____
_____
VIDEO TITLE: _____
_____
_____

What did you learn?
_____
_____
_____
_____
_____
_____

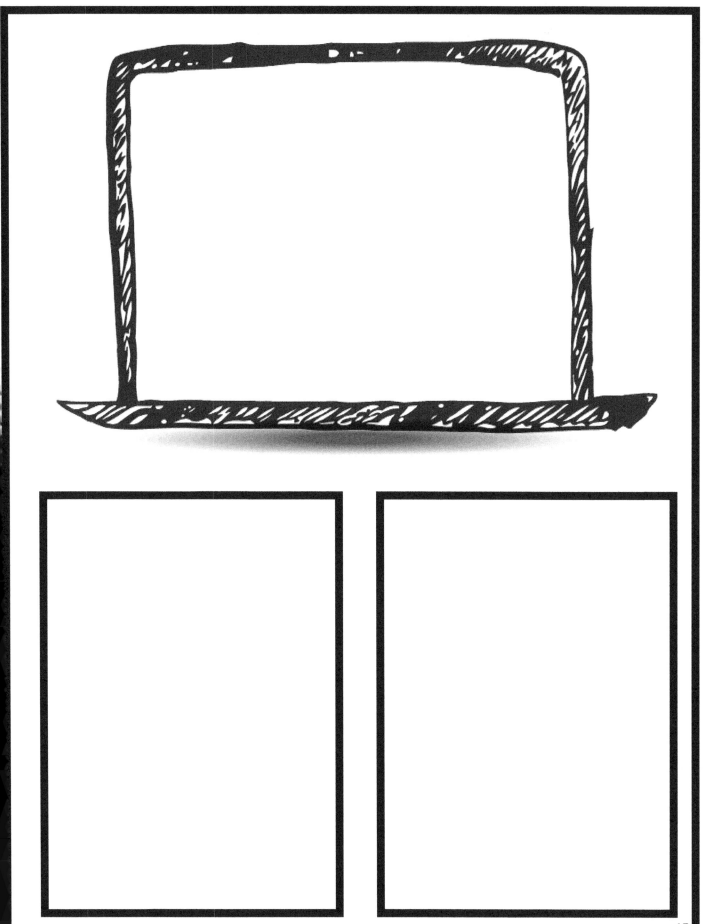

IRISH CUISINE

What do Irish people love to eat?

Can you list **5** of the most
popular Irish dishes?

1. _____
2. _____
3. _____
4. _____
5. _____

Draw your favorite Irish food

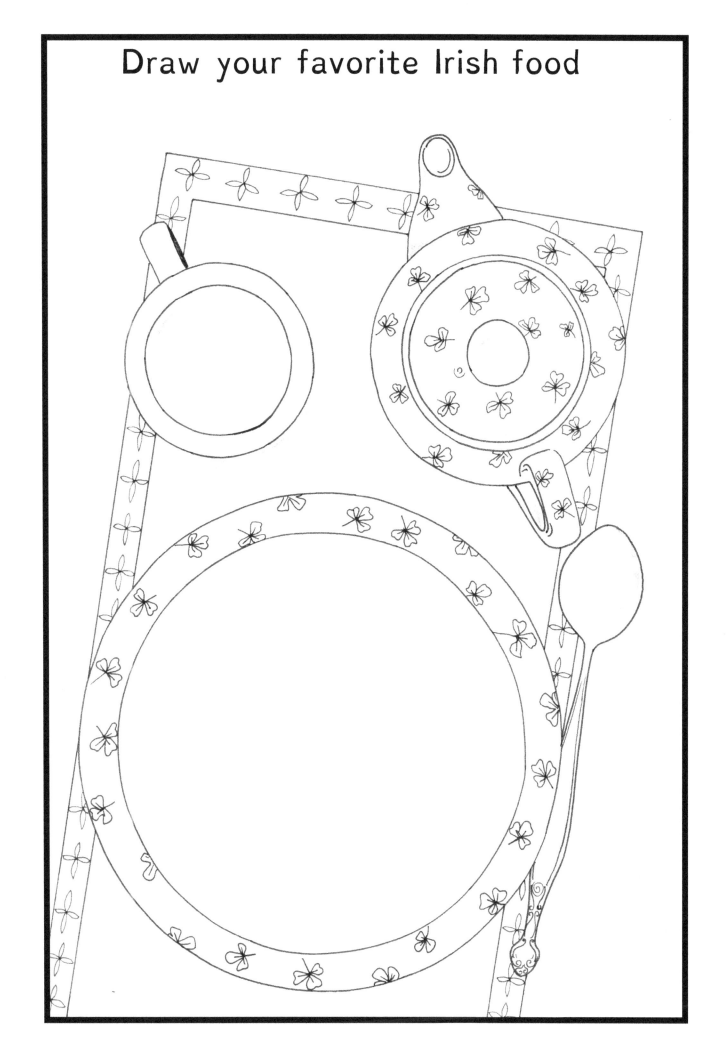

Find a Recipe From
IRELAND
TITLE:

_____

Ingredients:

_____   _____

_____   _____

_____   _____

_____   _____

_____   _____

Instructions:

_____

_____

_____

_____

_____

_____

_____

_____

_____

Step by Step Food Prep:

1	2
3	4
5	6

DRAW THE FOOD THAT YOU PREPARED!

RATE THE RESULTS!
1, 2, 3, 4, 5

Color the words that best describe your food:

DELICIOUS
YUMMY
TASTY
GREAT
DELIGHTFUL
OKAY
BLAH!
GROSS
YUCKY
DISGUSTING
STINKY
ICKY

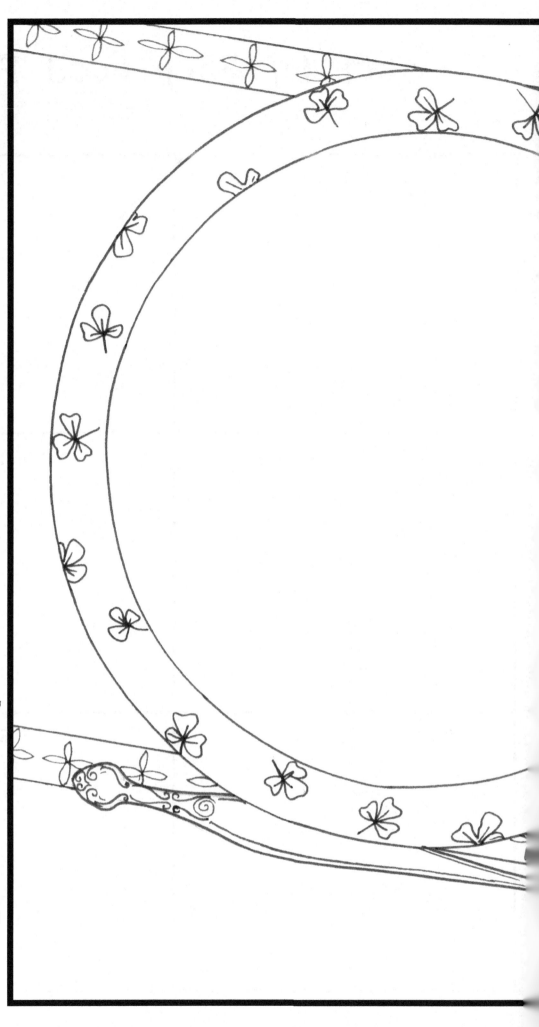

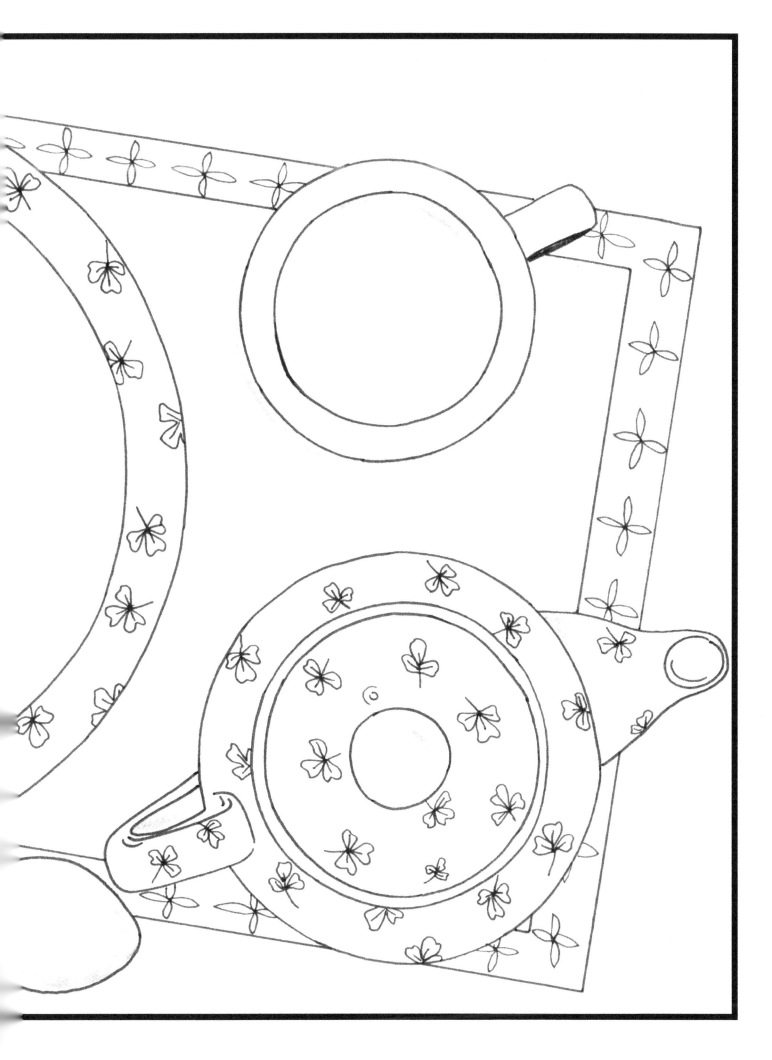

What to Do in Ireland

Create a **COMIC STRIP** showing your dream adventure!

LEARNING TIME

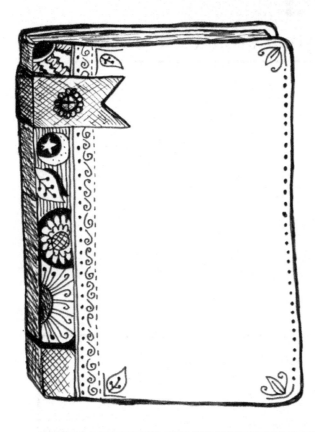

READ A BOOK AND WATCH A VIDEO ABOUT A FAMOUS PERSON

BOOK TITLE:_____
_____
VIDEO TITLE: _____
_____
_____

Write 3 Interesting Biography Facts

_____
_____
_____
_____
_____
_____

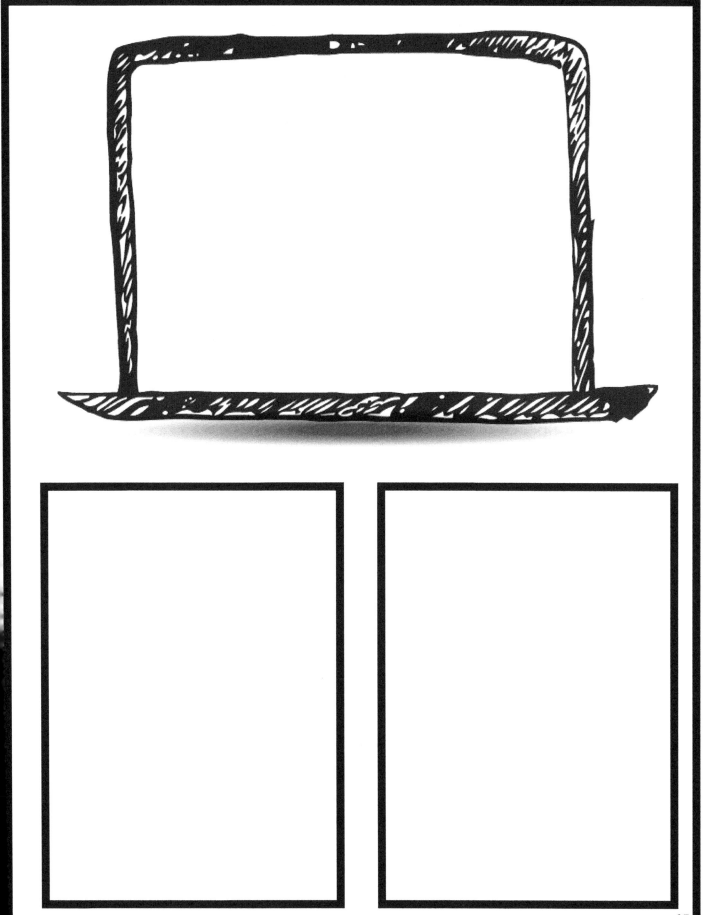

IRELAND

Fashion in the City

_____

_____

_____

MODERN STYLES

Draw yourself dressed like a stylish Irish person:

Color The Traditional Costume:

Trace and color this traditional Female Irish costume

Trace and color this traditional male Irish costume

IRELAND HISTORY

Write about a Historic Event

LEARNING TIME

READ A BOOK AND WATCH A VIDEO ABOUT NATURE & WILDLIFE

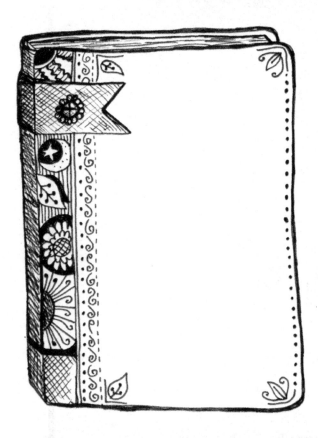

BOOK TITLE:_____
_____
VIDEO TITLE: _____
_____
_____

Notes:
_____
_____
_____
_____
_____
_____

What Animals Live in Ireland?
Can you List ten?

1. _____
2. _____
3. _____
4. _____
5. _____
6. _____
7. _____
8. _____
9. _____
10. _____

Draw each of the animals

37

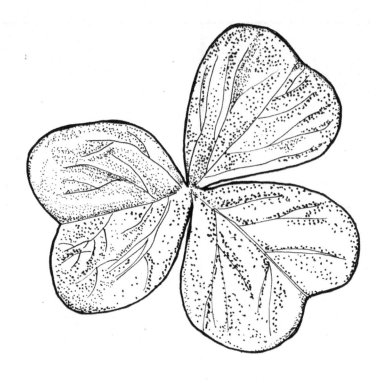

PLANTS IN IRELAND

Can you list ten flowers or trees found in Ireland?

1. _____
2. _____
3. _____
4. _____
5. _____
6. _____
7. _____
8. _____
9. _____
10. _____

Draw each of the plants

HISTORY OF MUSIC IN IRELAND

Write about a famous Irish musician:

_____

_____
_____
_____
_____
_____
_____

What instrument did he/she play?

_____

Can you draw it?

A NATIONAL INSTRUMENT

To hear traditional music from this country listen to
Travel Dreams Geography— Around the World in **14** Songs

Track Number & Song Name:
01-Ireland – The Dance of Heather Hills

IRISH ART & ENTERTAINMENT

Read a book or watch a documentary about art and entertainment in Ireland

Write down 5 interesting things you learned :

1. _____

_____

2. _____

_____

3. _____

_____

4. _____

_____

5. _____

_____

Draw or doodle in Irish Style

Write down a quote or a Lyric From a Famous Irish poem or Song

_____

_____

_____

_____

_____

_____

_____

_____

_____

_____

_____

_____

_____

_____

HISTORY OF TRANSPORTATION IN IRELAND

Find 3 interesting facts about Irish transportation

1. _____
_____
_____

2. _____
_____
_____

3. _____
_____
_____

Use your imagination and add something to this picture.

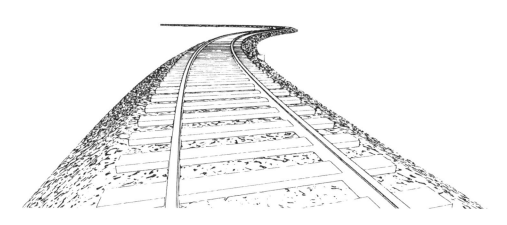

Write a short story about this picture

_____

_____

_____

_____

_____

_____

_____

_____

IRISH INVENTIONS

Read a book or watch a documentary about your favorite Irish inventor:

_____

Write down 5 interesting things about his/her life:

1._____
_____

2._____
_____

3._____
_____

4._____
_____

5._____
_____

Write down 3 Irish inventions that changed the world:

1. _____

2. _____

3. _____

DraW your Favorite IriSH iNVeNtioN

IRISH SPORTS

Read a book or watch a documentary about your favorite Irish Sport:

_____

Write down 5 interesting things about this sport

1. _____

_____

2. _____

_____

3. _____

_____

4. _____

_____

5. _____

_____

Draw your Favorite Irish Sport

IRISH HOMES
Write about a family tradition in Ireland

_____

_____

_____

_____

IRISH TRADITIONS
Draw some traditional Irish décor elements

Trace & Color
A TRADITIONAL IRISH HOME

Design Your Own
IRISH HOME

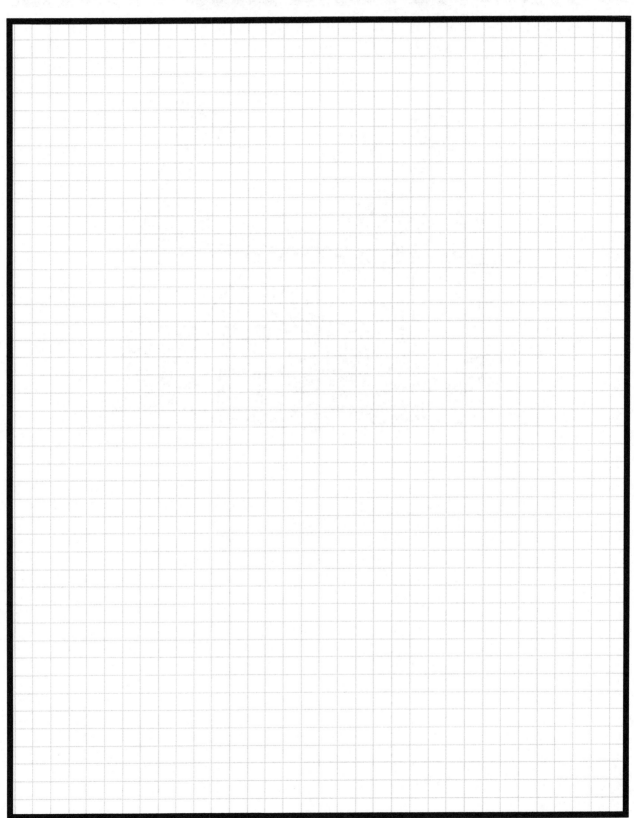

Find and color in the hidden objects

LEARNING TIME

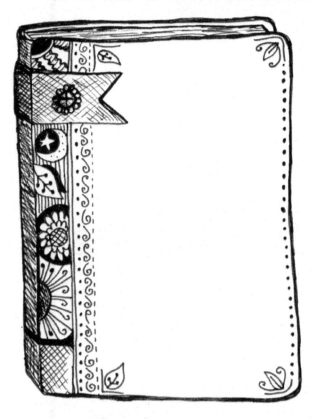

READ A BOOK AND WATCH A VIDEO ABOUT TOURISM & TRAVEL

BOOK TITLE:_____

_____

VIDEO TITLE: _____

_____

_____

Notes:

_____

_____

_____

_____

_____

_____

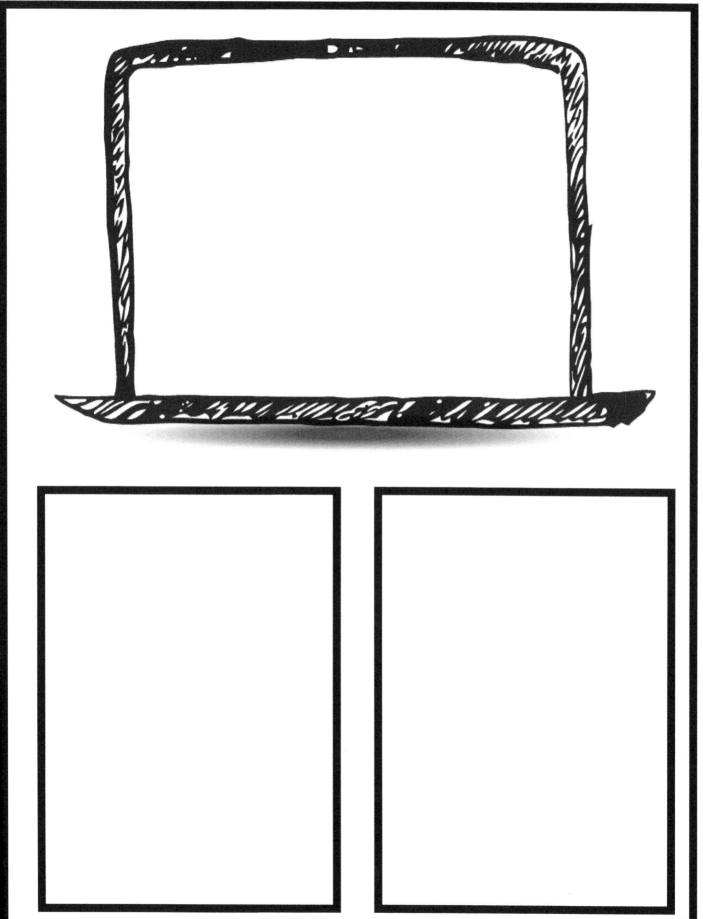

PLAN A TRIP TO THE CAPITAL OF IRELAND

- - - - - -

Who are you going with?

_____

What are you taking with you?

_____

How long is your trip?

_____

What do you want to see or visit?

_____

PLAN YOUR TRIP
What to Do in Dublin

Five Things to Know
when Traveling to
IRELAND

1 _____

2 _____

3 _____

4 _____

5 _____

What to Say

Create a **COMIC STRIP** using six Irish phrases:

CREATIVE WRITING

Write a story about an imaginary trip to Ireland

Illustrate your Story

Do It Yourself
HOMESCHOOL
JOURNALS
BY THE THINKING TREE, LLC

FunSchoolingBooks.com

DyslexiaGames.com

Contact Us: jbrown@DyslexiaGames.com

THE Thinking TREE

PUBLISHING COMPANY

Sarah Janisse Brown

Made in the USA
Las Vegas, NV
02 June 2021